Tattered
Sails

VERLA KAY

illustrated by
DAN ANDREASEN

G. P. Putnam's Sons

Thomas, Edward,
Mary Jane,
Noses pressing,
Windowpane.

London crowded,
Choked with crime.
Clogged with noises,
Sooty grime.

Parents talking,
Making plans.
Children helping,
Packing pans.

Sacks of clothing,
Work tools, stacked.
Livestock, baggage,
Loaded, packed.

Harbor, galleon,
Captain, crew.
Sails unfurling,
Ocean blue.

Canvas billows,
Salty breeze.
Water glistens,
Azure seas.

Crowded quarters,
Candle lamp.
Musty blankets,
Clothing, damp.

Windy weather,
Pitching decks.
Children seasick,
Craning necks.

Hardtack dwindles,
Fresh fish sought.
Long lines, fishing,
"Nothing caught."

Thomas, Edward,
Mary Jane,
Stomachs growling,
Groan, complain.

Tainted water,
Slimy vats.
Wormy biscuits,
Lice and rats.

Storm clouds gather,
Driving rain.
High winds howling,
HURRICANE!

Battened hatches,
Barrels, rolled.
Tattered sails,
Leaky hold.

Seagulls soaring,
Fragrant air.
Soft breeze, balmy,
Weather, fair.

Misty vista,
Shady grove.
Rocky shoreline,
Sheltered cove.

Sea legs wobble,
Shaky feet.
Thatched roofed houses,
Pilgrims greet.

One room cabin,
Rush beds, soft.
Greased cloth windows,
Ladder, loft.

Mother resting,
Baby born.
Local natives,
Sharing corn.

Thomas, Edward,
Mary Jane,
Carting water,
Planting grain.

No more noisy,
Crowded street,
Crime-filled alley,
Sooty sleet.

Children laughing—
Leather ball,
Wooden cradle,
Corn husk doll.

Freedom, fresh air,
Hard work, play.
Family gathers,
Kneels to pray.

To my beautiful daughter, Portia,
for all the joy she's given me through the years —V. K.

AUTHOR'S NOTE

People came to America in the early 1600s for many reasons. Some came because they had no choice (England sent many shiploads of prisoners to the New World in order to rid their jails of criminals); others were searching for religious freedom. Some were fleeing crowded conditions, lack of work, and pestilence. The family in this story came for a combination of those reasons, mainly to build a better life for themselves.

I was astounded when my research turned up the Farmans, who sailed from London to Boston in July of 1635 on a ship called the *James*, with children named Thomas, Mary, and Ralph—almost identical to the Thomas, Mary Jane, and Edward of my fictional family! It was very exciting to discover this real family that mirrored my fictional one so closely. Mr. Farman became the town crier and sexton of the village of Ipswich, but the future of my fictional family has been left up to your imagination.

Text copyright © 2001 by Verla Kay. Illustrations copyright © 2001 by Dan Andreasen. All rights reserved.
This book, or parts thereof, may not be reproduced in any form without permission in writing from the publisher.
G. P. Putnam's Sons, a division of Penguin Putnam Books for Young Readers, 345 Hudson Street, New York, NY 10014.
G. P. Putnam's Sons, Reg. U.S. Pat. & Tm. Off. Published simultaneously in Canada. Printed in Hong Kong by South
China Printing Co. (1988) Ltd. Designed by Gunta Alexander. Text set in Caslon Antique.
The artist scanned traditional graphite drawings and a custom palette of textured oil paints into the computer.
He filled in the sketches with the palette and printed them out. Next he painted on the printouts and added
detail using charms as stencils and carved erasers as stamps.

Library of Congress Cataloging-in-Publication Data   Kay, Verla. Tattered sails / Verla Kay; illustrated by Dan Andreasen.
p. cm.   Summary: Illustrations and simple rhyming text depict the journey of a family from London to the Massachusetts
Bay Colony in 1635. [1. Voyages and travels—Fiction. 2. United States—History—Colonial period, ca. 1600–1775—Fiction.
3. Stories in rhyme.] I. Andreasen, Dan, ill. II. Title. PZ8.3.K225Tat 2001 [E]—dc21 99-19249   ISBN 0-399-23345-8
1 3 5 7 9 10 8 6 4 2
First Impression